FABER & FABER has published children's books since 1929. Some of our very first publications included Old Possum's Book of Practical Cats by T. S. Eliot starring the now world-famous Macavity, and The Iron Man by Ted Hughes. Our catalogue at the time said that 'it is by reading such books that children learn the difference between the shoddy and the genuine'. We still believe in the power of reading to transform children's lives.

About the Author

Laura Dockrill is an English performance poet, author, illustrator and short story writer. Laura was born and grew up in Brixton. She is the author of the Darcy Burdock series; two YA novels, *Lorali* and *Aurabel*; as well as a number of adult poetry collections. *My Mum's Growing Down* is her first poetry collection for children.

About the Illustrator

David Tazzyman lives near Leicester with his partner and three sons. He likes drawing a lot. He illustrated the bestselling and multiple award-winning Mr Gum series, and Waterstone's bestselling picture book *You Can't Take an Elephant on the Bus*.

My Mum's Growing Down

Laura Dockrill

illustrated by David TAZZYMAN

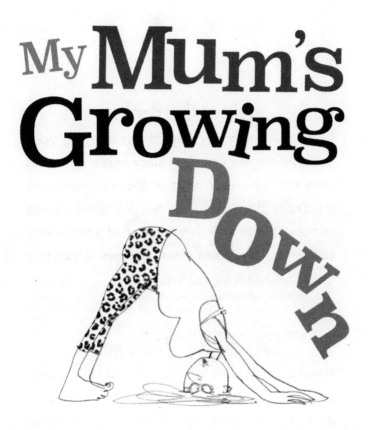

ff

FABER & FABER

For my mum x

DT

First published in 2017
by Faber & Faber Ltd
Bloomsbury House
74–77 Great Russell Street
London WC1B 3DA

Typeset by Faber & Faber
Printed in the UK by CPI Group (UK) Ltd, Croydon

The right of Laura Dockrill and David Tazzyman to be identified as author
and illustrator of this work respectively has been asserted in accordance
with Section 77 of the Copyright, Designs and Patents Act 1988

A CIP record for this book is available from the British Library

ISBN 978-0-571-33506-0

For my own grown down

LD

Contents

Part One, Me:

Part Two, Mum:

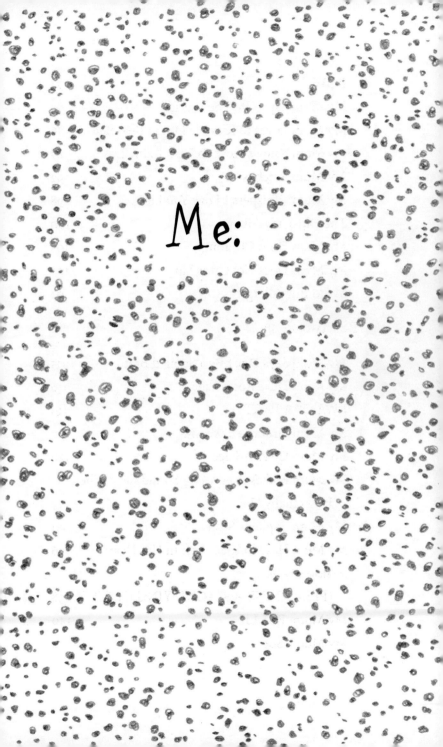

Me:

My Mum's Growing Down

There's something I must tell you since my
   teacher will not listen,
I wonder if you've heard of my mother's
   s-t-r-a-n-g-e condition,
It is a bit unusual; I can't *fake* to be proud,
I'm sure your mum's a grown up,
But . . .

My mum's growing DOWN!

She says 'I've worked so hard for years and
   I deserve a rest!'
As she scribbles with crayons and pours
   custard down her dress,
She's dangling from the banister with her
   head upside-down!
Does your mum do this?
Help!

My mum's growing DOWN!

Mum's as old as a T. Rex but she never acts
her age,
And I can't take her anywhere as she always
misbehaves!
She looks like a flamingo, a sparkle disco
clown
Is your mum growing up?
Because . . .

My mum's growing DOWN!

She eats chocolate cake for breakfast, drinks
milkshakes instead of tea,
She draws on the walls with lipstick and
blames the mess on me!
She cries her wrinkly eyes out if she can't
wear her ballgown!
The house is crazy chaos!
Since

My mum's growing DOWN!

She seeks out the vegetables I've hidden in
   her mash
Then with **PERMANENT** marker, she
   gives herself a 'tache
'Let's pretend I'm a *dad* today when we go
   into town!'
Not another day of this . . .
Please . . .

My mum's growing DOWN!

She says, 'I've taken care of you for years,
   now *you* take care of *me*!
Make me a jelly-pie sandwich please, then
   lullaby me to sleep.'
I just wish she'd do the dishes instead of
   '*chilling out*'
Whilst your mum's making dinner . . .
Guess what . . .

My mum's growing DOWN!

She likes to play mermaids in the bath, bake
cookies up from scratch
And she stomps in the supermarket like a
spoiled brat
If I don't buy *that cereal* she throws herself
on the ground
And I'm supposed to be the kid!
But OH NO . . .

My mum's growing DOWN!

Mum says 'Life's too short for boring-ness,
it's time we had some **FUN**!'
As she sprays me in the face with her brand
new water gun
She's forgotten the word 'quiet' so her voice is
BOOMING loud . . .
And I just want some '*me*' time
AS IF . . .

My mum's growing DOWN!

She shoves baked beans up her nose, blows
  bubbles in her juice
'That looks like POO!' she screams
  as you eat your chocolate mousse
She lies on her back and sees rainbows in
  the clouds
Whilst your mum is a *proper* mum

My mum's growing DOWN!

Now there's glitter in the toothpaste,
  bunny ears on her head
A gross collection of bogies wiped
  underneath her bed
She's learning to play the trumpet;
  she carries a hula-hoop around
Can you see what I'm dealing with here?

My mum's growing DOWN!

I apologise to passers-by, this is just what
Mum's like
As she rides behind on a skateboard tied to
the backseat of my bike
And if a *normal* mum makes you *normal*
then I guess I'm out of luck
Because all of Mum's growing down is
making **me grow up!**

But '*a little touch of playfulness is what will
keep you young*'
So I wouldn't switch this naughty parent for
another one,
Even though she's so annoying and stands
out from the crowd
There's never a dull day when . . .

My mum's growing DOWN!

My Mum Has Hair On Her Head and This Is What It's Like . . .

Mangled, tangled,
neck is strangled,
spider leg dangles
on a string.

My mum's hair
is like Rapunzel's
undles of bundle,
what shall we do with it?

Knit a scarf
for a giraffe,
a hammock
for a swing,

sew a drawbridge
for a moat,
loop ropes for
wrestling,

thatch a net
to catch
a pet,
crotchet a field of wheat,
web a bed
a pillow and spread
and a set
of hairy sheets!

Mum says she loves it
all winding and wrapping,
spilt end snapping
and climbing
the walls . . .

But I cannot stand it
all crawling and slacking
and making me late for school.

It's a storage cupboard,
a handbag
to rummage,
like Medusa's snatching
snakes,

a beehive,
a tidal wave,
a nit-infested cave.

The brush
is afraid,
been missing for days and
we're all out of conditioner

and the scissors
bend,
the hairdryer
plays sick for pretend
and nobody can find the
the hairdresser!

The rough
scruff of trouble
is a weed-breeding jungle
that looks like the fluff in the hoover!

Like dressing gown
tassels
you would NOT want to battle
as you'd always end up
as the loser!

To bulk it up
she's even used bread,
a roll of baguette
on top of her head!

Grubby as
sewage,
you cannot
comb through it
so you're better off staying
in bed!

It's like her hair has muscles
as she
does the daily struggle
of wrestling with this
halo boss,

it's bed head
or wind swept,
this head
is a flea bed
and is best to be
SHAVED OFF!

My Mum Is a Gamer

My mum is a gamer,
she sleeps with one eye wide,
a balaclava on her head, control pad by
   her side . . .

My mum is a gamer,
a solider in disguise,
a superhero pirate, an undercover spy.

My mum is a gamer,
she has to be the best,
holed up in the dining room is Sergeant Mama's
    nest.

My mum is a gamer
in a dystopian apocalypse
with a bulletproof vest, grenade in her fist.

My mum is a gamer,
roaring orders from above,
she wears those big black boots now and a
    pair of fingerless gloves.

My mum is a gamer,
her clothes are camouflage –
'I don't know if the sofa's real, Son, or simply
    a mirage!'

My mum is a gamer,
unprepared to lose,
spitting out directions on her new
    hands-free Bluetooth.

14

My mum is a gamer,
deep sea diving with harpoons,
a first aid box if she gets crossed, the
    boss of her platoon.

My mum is a gamer,
steers the wheel of a plane,
army tank, submarine or 400-foot crane.

My mum is a gamer,
crawling supermarket aisles,
sipping water from the trenches
    groaning 'one more mile.'

My mum is a gamer,
the teachers all stare scared
as she charges in to collect me like
    a mammoth grizzly bear,

My mum is a gamer,
my friends think she's so cool
as she challenges them to a round
    and always beats them all

My mum is a gamer,
biting bullets for a snack,
shouting **'ATTACK FROM THE
BACK!'** then launching for the cat!

My mum is a gamer
in a 3D fantasy,
lost in the maze for days in the dream
    of our flat screen.

My mum is a gamer,
baking us lasagna
then tipping it down herself, wailing
**'I've been SHOT,
    commander!'**

My mum is a gamer,
it's now her full-time job,
but I might do her a favour and switch
    the power off.

My Mum Does Not Dress Like a Mum and That's Good

feather boa
veil of lace
silver bangles
dolly face
purple boots
sparkle shoes
peep toe
velvet throw
king-like cape
cactus shirt
dungarees
splash
in dirt . . .
dress
like a movie star
dress like a
biscuit

dress like a camper van
with loads of stuff in it
squeeze into
my clothes
forget about the seams
dress like the sunshine
dress like a dream
celebrate the alien
dress to stand out
glitter on your cheeks
like a freak
illuminate the town,
rags, drags and
rucksacks
glitz, shine and dazzle
wiggle
like a jiggle
of streaky bacon on the frazzle,

multi-coloured leggings
and netted fish tights
don't bother with the shape
no
don't bother with the size
just dress like a mess she says
a mess
that hurts the eyes
leopard print leotard
sequin waistcoat
Mum dances with a broomstick
a mop-top bloke
swishing like milk
in satin and silk
leather jacket
with the pockets
collars with the frills
diamond cuffs
or green camo
neon trim ra-ra skirt!
Mama can be anything
my chameleon iguana
but I think Mum looks her best . . .
just in her bobbly old pajamas

My Mum Wants a Bedtime Story

'*O*nce upon a . . .'
Mum begins to read
but then she stops her place
within the page
and takes a look at me.

'Can't you read *me* a story?
It's always this way round.
I want to know how it
feels to lie in bed
whilst a story of **yours** pours out.'

'But Mum, *YOU'RE* the mum
you're meant to read to **ME**.'
But Mum only raises a brow
and grunts,
'well, that rule is just silly.'

'FINE.' I groan, 'just this once
I'll read to you before bed

but don't get too used to this set-up,
Mum,
this weird idea in your head.'

'YES!' She squeals
and shoves me out the duvet
that is **MINE**
'Oi!' I bark,
but she just laughs,
and nestles down all nice.

'Once upon a . . . '
'BORING!' She roars,
'not this one again
it's got no plot line
no twists, no turns
no curves or swerves or bends.'

I roll my eyes and
choose another from the shelf
'NO! NO!' She caws across the room,
'please can't you choose something else?'

'This one?'

'BOO! NO!
It's got no soul or bones or body or any heart
it's got a terrible ending
that is nearly as awful
as the start.'

'Well, what about . . . '
'NO! Put that down, I
can't stand that ghastly thing,
the words are an insult to the paper
and it's basically about **NOTHING.'**

'OK then, Mum, you're making this tough
if you're just going to lie
there and make a fuss,
why don't you choose a story
that isn't boring,
something that **YOU** love?'

Mum wriggles down
and softly smiles
and closes her eyes
and thinks for a while . . .

'What about the one
with the *whale*
and the *MAGIC TAIL*
and the **AIR BALLOON**
and the old cartoons
and the bedtime jar
with the hand that **bites**
and salad dressing
that comes alive at night
and the *witch's* nose
and the GOBLIN eyes
and the s-t-r-a-w-b-e-r-r-y hair
and the **big surprise**
when the ALIENS land
and the *serpent* lurks
and the VAMPIRE
that **breaks** the **genie curse**
or the **horse** with **wings**
or the **frog that sings**
and the *missing key*
and the t r a m p o l i n e
that every time you bounce
grants *chocolate treats!*

The MAD PRiNCESS
with the **secret sword
and the old**
trap   door
in the wooden floor
or the *sequin* tree
that sees everything
or the talking . . . cabbage
the dancing ferret . . .
you **MUST** know the one?
Oh, move over,
Son,
it will be more fun
if you let *me* tell it.'

My Mum Just Does Yoga Now These Days . . .

*D*ownward Facing Dog
carpet eating hog

Crow Pose
floorboard meeting nose

The Rooted Tree
two bruised knees

The Cobra
a cow on the sofa

The Eagle
really, is more of a seagull
swooping down
stealing chips from people

The Cat
a doormat

The Scorpion
a slug . . . (Yes I know it doesn't rhyme. Stop
    being so clever.)

The Horse, Camel and Hare
is Mum on all fours roaring like a bear
with one foot on the banister dangling off the stairs
screaming 'SOMEONE, QUICK, GET ME DOWN
                    FROM HERE!'

and that just leaves *Child's Pose*
a simple bow to the sun
until I get flattened quick
by Mum's yoga bum.

My Mum Is my Dad

My mum is a mum
but also a dad
My mum is my mum
but also my dad
I know it's confusing
and a sounds a bit mad
how can one parent
be a mum and a dad?
(The word mum and dad
together
makes the word
MAD
anyway so . . .
that's what I have – a MAD)
don't want to overcomplicate
get mushy or sad
but I *definitely* have
both a mum and a dad
the love of a
bajillion parents

smushed into one
the heart of a
gatrillion parents
love me at once

through her
eyes
and smile
I can walk any mile
I thrive
on more love
than any one child

Mum does everything
people say a dad 'should'
she can do anything any dad could

she stands up for me
and puts me on her shoulders
she starts sentences with
'when you are older'
she loves me to death
and could squeeze the bones
right out of my flesh

I am her best
she drinks beer
and gives me advice
and I am loved not once
but **'GREEDILY'** twice
and if ever people ask
'where's your dad gone?'
I say 'nowhere'
and point at my
mum.

I say 'nowhere.'
And point at my mum.

My Mum Wants to Go To the 'Movies!' Hooray. (in a sarcastic voice)

Stop calling it the *movies*,
Mum,
stop calling it the *movies*.

It's called the 'CINEMA',
Mum,
why'd you keep calling it the *movies*?

Do you have to wear that ugly skirt,
Mum?
It's way too big for you,

you trip up when you wear it,
Mum,
and drag me down with you!

AND
do you have to make

those awkward jokes,
Mum,
at the kiosk bit?

And moan about the prices,
Mum,
every time we make a visit?

Do you have to get *three* popcorns,
Mum,
and a hot dog too?

Do you need *every* flavour of ice cream,
and that weird slushy drink that's blue?

Do you have to already start eating it
and **crunch** it the queue?
You haven't paid for it yet,
Mum,
everybody's looking at you!

Do you have to lose our tickets,
MUM?

Do you have to **RUN** down the stairs?
Do you have to **SCREAM** my name
OUT LOUD
when those kids from school are there?
Did you not see the big mirrors,
MUM,
that cover the walls and ceiling?
Did you have to wear that
   TOO BIG SKIRT,
can't you see it unravelling?
Did you have to let your skirt fall **OFF,**
MUM,
in front of all those mirrors?
You tumbled in the rumble of the stampede
   at the pictures!
And **ALL** those kids from school were there,
MUM,
and strangers point and snigger
and all over every big screen
was the flash of

MUM'S BIG KNICKERS!

I flush red with embarrassment,
almost have a heart attack.

Why didn't you pull up your skirt Mum?

She said,

'I didn't want to lose the snacks.'

My Mum's Hands Don't Ever Meet Soap

Mum's hands
are as **rough** as sand
and covered in **dirt** and **mud**

leave a **yuck** trail
behind each nail
that look like **vile black slugs**

Mum's fingers
are like diggers
that **grab** and **drag** and **rake**

in the garden
in the larder
then she'll want to *'build'* a cake

Mum will use a hose,
feed a goat,
sneeze out an ocean and wipe her nose

Mum will do *plumbing*
take out the rubbish
and **never** go near the sink

she'll play with the dog
squeeze a few spots
with fingertips raw and pink

like **stinky** old prawns
her gross filthy paws
snatch and point and flick

nails like a saw
banana claws
are not ones you'd like to **lick**

she will make a shed
scratch her head
and then pick a grain from her tooth

chop garlic and onion,
put cream on her bunion
and then want to come near **YOU!**

She rubs her feet
then makes the tea
and doesn't understand

why I love my mum the most
but never dare come close
to **those hands!**

One Pot

Never

say you're hungry

OUT LOUD

to a person that

loves you

cos they will feed you

up

like

a **BALLOON** that could

POP

like wiping the ocean

with one tissue

it's always too much

for you to mop

up

it's chilli

HOT

and often

GOT

stuff
in I can't
quite chew.

It's brown
or red
and never plain
and one
pot never tastes the same
so no point in asking
for it again
because she'll say
it's the same pot
but it's not.
It's a bit of **this**
and a LOT of that
a **dash** of this
and a **splash** of that
season
spices
onion
dices
or if she feels posh – darling,
shallots.
Fruit of tomatoes
juice the window
paprika down her frock
a curry paste

she will not waste
never a taste
– the **LOT!**
Only Mum knows
how to make a house a home
with a swirl of something secret
and although I moan
of Mum's one pot episodes
I just shut up and eat it.

My Mum Wants To Go To the 'Movies!' AGAIN! Hooray. Oh, Great. (in a really sarcastic voice)

Do you have to hold my hand,
Mum?
Everyone might see.
I don't care *if it's dark*,
Mum,
Stop holding hands with me!

That's not even *our* seat,
Mum,
shhh – you're in the wrong one.
Yes, I know *you paid like everyone else*
but you have to move along!

Stop shouting at the trailers,
Mum,
stop burping up slurps of your Coke.
Don't throw popcorn at the old man's head,
he doesn't get the joke!

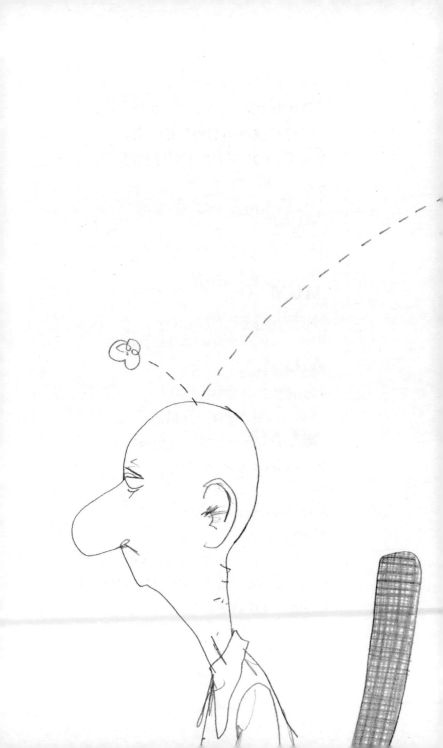

Stop laughing at the sad bits,

Mum,

and causing an absolute riot!

Do you have to tell her to get out the way?

Can't you just be quiet?

Do you have to cry on my shoulder,

MUM?

Don't use my arm as a snot rag!

Stop wailing like a walrus,

MUM,

this bit isn't even sad!

Stop placing crisps on that kid's hair,

MUM,

leave the girl's sweets alone!

Wait . . . did you just do a fart,

MUM?

No wonder we're on our own!

My Mum Is a Bird

My mum is a magpie
with a sharp eye for treasure
a twinkle in the ground's wrinkle
all claws and black feathers
and
precious stone glinting
and bright jewels that glitter
under the moonbeams
of silver night shimmer

sometimes she's a parrot
a noisy chatterbox
tongue quick as an arrow
in a rainbow splash frock

although maybe she's an owl
that's wise and sincere
with a head full of stories
to whisper in ears

but then she's a goose
gaggling around
squabbling with her squad
pecking coins from the ground

or she's a humble hen
that keeps me in check
that nurtures with motherness
now and then lays an egg

oh my, she's a swan
elegant and proud
but sometimes she goes ostrich
stuffs her head in the ground

some mornings she's a rooster
bellowing down the house
or as common as a pigeon
strutting to town

Mum's a yellow canary
when she's up baking bread
retelling her secrets
cackling off her head

she's a parakeet in the sun
can be a winter crow
cheap thrills just like a budgie,
kind robin in the snow

all mums fly like sparrows
but mine's as rare as the dodo
and when she migrates I'll follow
wherever the old bird goes

Mum Does the Museum (sigh)

Mum says,

'I want to learn about history
and how baby penguins sleep.
I want to learn how the world began
and how a starfish eats!
You'll never learn an anything
in that room of yours.
Let's go to the museum,
let's get ourselves outdoors.'

The Tube was a nightmare.
Mum wanted to *'make friends'*.
She sat next to a stranger
and said, 'Where you off to, then?'
She reads papers over shoulders,
pretends to pick her nose,
swings from bars like a monkey
and ribbits like a toad.

I pretend not to know her
at the museum door,
but her screeching squeals of **EXCITEMENT**
patter echoes on the walls.
'I don't know about you . . .'
she screams,

'BUT I CAN'T **WAIT** TO EXPLORE!'

I say, 'No stealing, Mum, OK?
This stuff is very precious.'
And she rolls her eyes at me
just so I know she's got the message.

All the signs say **NO PHOTOS!**
and read **DO NOT TOUCH!**
But my mum's rolling solo
and doesn't listen much.
She's sashaying like she owns the place,
bossing the staff with an antique spear.

She beats her chest like a gorilla
and yells **'I just LOVE it here!'**
The guard confiscates her camera
She calls him a 'fruit bat'!

Then exchanges clothes with a viking
and pulls down a caveman's pants!
She lipstick kisses a stuffed goose
and gathers up a flock
of kids that crack up at her jokes:
'OI! Let's rob the gift shop!'

I get so embarrassed
I have to run away.
I hide behind a big bald man
eating cake in the café.
I wait there for ages
pretending I'm not with anyone,
but the café is so boring . . .
I bet Mum's out having fun.
I should go back and get her now,
but the museum's shutting down.
'We're closing for the night', they say,
but Mum is nowhere to be found!

I start to panic terribly –
WHERE HAS MY MUM GONE?

She's not by the butterflies
or the yellowing dinosaur bones.
I run all around the building
my heart **SMASHING** in my ribs –
my mum has gone missing
and the building is so **BIG!**
I leave a message with this guy
and I begin to feel sick.
Mum's **REAL** name goes out on a speaker.
I bite my nails down to the quick,
but Mum's been waiting at the front desk.
She's been worrying too –
'I think I was a bit naughty
and might've embarrassed you.'

We walk along the river.
We eat hot chips with our hands.
Mum says, 'I got you a present, Son,
it's a pair of caveman pants.'

My Mum Loves to Complain in Restaurants

$\int$he cannot help herself,
there's always got to be a **CATCH**,
no matter **WHAT IS ON THE PLATE**
my mum will send it **BACK**;
the steak is never rare enough,
no browning on the **FAT**,
there are *green* things in the peas please,
the bread so burnt it's **BLACK!**
Why is the butter so **salty**, then?
Why are there **WORMS** in the spag bol?
Am I meant to cut this soup *myself*?
You call *this* a sausage roll?
The sauce is just too drippy, see?
The egg is just **TOO SOFT.**
Is pasta meant to be this **slippery?**
Is cheese meant to be this **OFF?**
(AND NO I *can't* eat this pie my friend it
    appears to be covered in . . . errr . . .
        ummm . . . COUGH!)

and there's a hair in my stew
– I know it looks like mine but it's not!
And I don't like the *feel* of the napkin.
May I *PLEASE* have my ice served **HOT?**
EUGH!
The plate is in a square shape.
You said fish *fingers*, they're more like *toes*
(oh, and now fish don't have toes *apparently* –
oh, you know it all I suppose!).
He's not even wearing a **CHEF HAT!**
Can I get the furniture to go?
When I say spicy I mean S-P-I-C-Y.
When I say large I mean **LARGE.**
I've asked you several times quite nicely
I want this free of charge!
I'm not paying for the burger
I'm not paying for the chips
I'm not paying for the sponge cake
so **DON'T** expect a tip!
NO I didn't eat it all . . .
my belly just likes to 'borrow'
This place is an absolute disgrace
I stuffed my face
but I'll be back tomorrow.

My Mum Attends Parents' Evening

I dread this day
in every way
the day
Mum gets *let* into school.

She'll STARE
and swear
without a care
you just can't prepare
at all.

She'll 'rock'
her 'frock'
with the too-low top
or the hippy smock
I bet

and walk the halls
like she owns the school

with a neck too tall
to forget
and she'll wave to mums
but they'll be the ones
whose sons
are not my friends.

And I'll just smile
whilst
Mum acts the child
and fake smile for pretend

with a blobble of spit
a flick of the wrist
she wipes chocolate off my cheek

her boiling hot lick
makes me feel sick
she's SO embarrassing.

'My son,' she'll start,
'is a genius at heart,
he just finds it hard
to express

he's just like **ME**
I have three degrees
and always achieve the
best.'

Teachers hit back
with fatal attack
pen ink so black
marks the sheets

and Mum's face contorts
like a shark's afterthought
and snorts
**'WHAT ON EARTH DO
    YOU MEAN?**

You think you're so smart
just because you teach art
you paint like a *fart*
if you ask me

behave like a **god**
because your job's in the pond
waiting for frogs to sprog

Miss Biology
you think you're so great
trying to be my mate
well, you're bang out of date
Mr History

No, I won't keep calm
get off my arm,'
as Mum whacks the alarm
with her handbag

and a riot is caused
as Mum, now on all fours,
crawls to the door
which slams with a bang

'I hate that place
they have no taste
it's a waste
they can't even teach!'

but deep down we know
my report would glow so
if Mum only let them speak.

Eyeball Roll

Mum's annoyed again.
Her face all smeared away.
Some is on her hand now.
Some swims down the drain.

Mum's all p'd off.
She tuts like a camel.
I find her worries in the sink
and teardrops on the flannel.

Mum's in a mood again.
She curls up in bed.
I make her a cup of tea
and leave it by her head.

I don't expect a thank you.
I don't expect a hi.
I don't expect what comes next
after we say goodnight.

Mum shouts *those* words at me
and scrubs and smokes and sleeps
and draws glasses and black teeth
on women in magazines.

Mum's tipped over the edge
with a cliff hanger for a spine
and her feelings are all hung out now
like knickers on the line.

Mum's eyeballs are rolling,
deep sighing out their sockets.
They spin like planets on the table
and into my small pockets.

Mum says it's one of those days
but the sky looks clear tomorrow.
You can't have sun without a storm
or joy without the sorrow.

My Mum Does Some Exaggerating

Mum exaggerates
to **double** the size
upgrades the truth
and multiplies
where it's **triple** the DANGER
unleash of the lies
where friends are **STRANGERS**
and mundane, **SURPRISE!**
It's **HUNDREDS** instead of
two
THOUSANDS instead of
one
it's never just a little bit
it's a **LOADED-ON-TOP-OF-IT**
TON
where the day is never ending
and the road is *oh   so   long*
and a normal HB pencil
is now a machine gun

and a twig becomes an **oak tree**

and a cat becomes a **fox**

and a tiny spot upon your cheek

is a bout of **chicken pox**

and you're not peckish

you are **STARVING**

and walking

is **MARCHING**

and a rain cloud

is a **twister**

and a **hurricane is starting**

and the weather is **BOILING**

and the lift takes *years*

and a tiny pair of tweezers

are a **set of garden shears**

and the candle is a **HOUSE FIRE**

and the mice are . . . errrr . . .

MONKEY BATS!

And your friends are **ALL** French

because one learnt the word *cravat*

and your teacher is a **MONSTER**

and the washing's **SOAKING** wet

the taxi driver is your chauffeur

and you **CANNOT** trust the vet
and the cakes are
HUUUUMMMMUUUNNNGGGOOUUUSSS
but the fruitcake was **VILE**
and Mum got concussion
from a violent nail file!
And the rumours are talking
and the puddles are **monsoons**
and your bedroom is a **c-r-a-w-l-i-n-g**
festering baboon

and the truth is a spindling web
of retelling crafty work

of loopholes in plot lines
and you're knee-deep in dirt
where the pigs are all flying
eyes are **bigger** than plates
and Mum's imagination is lying
but what a good tale it makes.

My Mum Can't

Can't cook
Can't clean
Can't sew up things
Not that mum with home-made treats

But watch her wobble around on stilts and own
the room like a queen

Can't fake
Can't make
Is always late
Never apologises for the time she takes

But watch her eradicate hate
Every day
With a curious smile on her face

Can't change
Won't change
Her unique ways

And shouldn't have to anyway

For she's My Mum and that's her way. So watch.
And be amazed.

Basically.

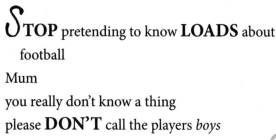

My Mum Pretends To Know Absolutely Loads About Football

S**TOP** pretending to know **LOADS** about
  football
Mum
you really don't know a thing
please **DON'T** call the players *boys*
and the pitch a *ring*

please don't call half-time
the *interval*
don't **SHOUT** at the TV
and that's a *tackle* not a *cuddle*
and that *teacher's* a referee

STOP pretending to know **LOADS** about
  football
Mum
it's not an audience
it's a *crowd*

STOP saying things like
'place a pass'
and booing really **LOUD**

STOP calling a free kick
'a lucky chance'
it's a hat trick not magic
and **STOP** saying your best bit
was the robot dance
and then grinning to yourself 'ha, classic'

STOP pretending to know **LOADS** about
football
Mum
he's their manager, not their *dad*
and that's called a header
not a *brainer* MUM
and **YES** footballers cry when they're sad

stop roaring
'YOU CAN DO IT!'
they can't hear you through the screen
and you can't just keep switching your support
to the winning team

STOP pretending to know loads about football
Mum
it's a penalty not a fine
no, not:
'it's already an hour and a half long
do they need **EXTRA** time?'

STOP wearing football boots please
Mum,
just put my football down
you don't know what you're doing
Mum
it's getting **E-M-B-A-R-R-A-S-S-I-N-G** now

where did you learn to do those kick-ups Mum?
maybe I misunderstood?
you might not know *loads* about football Mum
but you're actually pretty good.

ROW

Y ou growl
too proud
you stand and
scowl
and throw
a tea towel
at my head
I shout in your face
and smash a plate
by mistake
but it just makes it worse
instead
and the place is a state
and full of hate
and the space
rots up with dread

I roar
at you
and claw

the door
and slam the
handle
to the floor
and tell you mean
things even more
ROAR ROAR ROAR!
but you only ignore
me
and I'll never believe that
you once adored me

and you threaten me
with what's to come
and challenge me
with who I've become
and forget a bit to use words like
love
as the seams of us fray,
today are
undone

and I'll call you
an old fool

and crawl
and trawl
the pits
for bits
of mean things
to bawl
and throw
like paper balls at you
that explode
like bombs
and hurt you
and turn out to be maybe not
    made of any kind of paper at all.

I kick the wall
I stomp the stairs
I scratch the hallway
with a chair
and I call you things
that spring from my
tongue
many mean words Mum
for which you are none.

And back to back
we swamp in the black
and block out our shadows
to war our attack
and it's *I* **HATE** *you, Mum*
well *I* **HATE** *you back, Son*
and the little rip between us
soon becomes a crack

in silence we slither
the mood murders our ears
I miss your soft voice
so
you kiss my tears
I'm sorry you say
I'm sorry too
I love you today
and always will do

after the rain
we wrap up on the sofa
in our normal way
with our normal coasters
and on goes the kettle

and down with the toaster
it will happen again
because it's supposed to
but it never breaks us
we only get closer.
So it happens again
because it's supposed to.

My Mum Says 'Oh, The World!'

Me:

The news came on by accident
I hated every second
I wanted to throw a stone
and make a hole
in the television
the noises were all scratchy there
and blurred my mind
and stole my vision
The news came on by accident
and I hated every second
The colours were all chalk
and grey
black, brown and sad
the voices were all angry there
and bossy and hatter mad
and people that didn't look
friendly
were pretending they weren't bad

but you could see they were evil Mum
and as cold as concrete slabs
I saw the newspaper in the shop
next to the lollipops
I thought of rotting teeth and disease
instead of butterscotch
The paper shouted words at me
of people without homes
where are all those people Mum?
where do those people
go?
Mum, I know you're not a normal mum
but I need to ask you why
the world can be so terrible and selfish at times
I need you to tell me why
the world is a lopsided
wonky
pair
of eyes
because I saw a newspaper in the shop
and it made me want to cry
will it be like this forever Mum
is this the best world we can find?

MUM:

Oh, the world
the beautiful wonderful world
that rolls and
revolves and
evolves
can you tell
that I really do love the world?
I love that we exist
even though I don't know why
we live on a planet
that hangs in the sky
dangling like a decoration
for a Christmas tree
on an invisible
thread
Oh, I love the world, me
I love that flowers sprout out of cracks in
concrete pavements
that people write love letters
and make art for no reason
that the world is like a show
and we are all actors
except we never get to go home.

I love that the sky holds back snow
as a treat
and never fails to be magic
I love it when people are kind
and curious
and that our brains understand music
I love that people
find the little things that make them engine on and
tick.

Oh, I love the world
when animals are free
and that nature makes cool things like cotton
and rice and gems and honey
I love that water comes from streams
and dreams are cooked up in our heads
I love that we invented chocolate spread
and that chickens can hatch eggs
and we tell stories to a friend
and can be remembered
and then heard on again.

Oh, I LOVE LOVE LOVE the world
that it rains in one place but not in another
that when you are sleeping
somebody else is awake
that we keep on turning
for turning's sake
and yes horrible things do happen, Son
and that is awful news to break
but there is so much left to live for
there's so much more to say
and you have to see the goodness
you have to swim in that
because otherwise if you don't
you'll end up going mad
for every baddie is a thousand goods
for every worm is a trillion fruit
for every door that shuts in your face
two more will open too.

And remember every single time
you accidently see the news
the bad stuff's the only stuff they show
the good stuff is in you.

My Mum Loves to Kiss Me
Out in Real Life

You don't need to kiss me
when you pick me up –
I know that you love me
by the fact you turned up.

I am not your husband!
I am not your wife!
SO PLEASE don't kiss me
out in real life!

My Mum Knows How To Do a Rainy Day

Windows
closed because the rain
smacks the glass
cars speed past
the dirty afternoon
it's us all day
cocooned
in the rooms
of our shell
that never tell
us how to feel
but cast a spell
of grey Sunday nights
or Monday's spite
that hole us in
all wrapped up tight
and I dread the hours
that drag   on   by
the slow motion rolling of
noon to night

there's no point in turning
taps on
or making the bed right
just instead hum along
until it's time to say goodnight . . .

But that's until I remember who
    I live with . . .

oh yeah, that's real, that's right . . .

'A whole day of fun
and who better to spend it
    with than your **MUM?'**

She grins a thin
sideways leaf of a smile
then dials her head up
like a child
toasting cheese
and squeezy **cream**
button popping
BELLY DREAM
spots and stripes

∞

burst at the seams
on the sofa's
trampoline
the mirror
steams
a happy face
bouncy ball
three-legged race
to the front door
we pound and pace
and limbo to our favourite place
make a picnic
pack a case
imagine we're on holiday
read a book
bake a cake
mosh until the whole
house shakes
hide and seek
takeaway
eaten off our knees
on trays
change our rooms
and firework **BOOM**

pots of paint
SHOOT to the moon
draw on chins
and tickling
eat a doughnut
without licking
prank call the neighbours
WAR with our thumbs

who knew I could have this much fun
with Mum?
Put on the radio
dance around for ages
and am secretly happy
that it happens to be raining

(can I also just tell you that raining is amazing
because potatoes are actually really so good and
if it doesn't rain how will we get chips?)

My Mum Retches

(*Please note* to perform this poem to it's utmost potential please rehearse and perfect your greatest impression of VOMITING and every time you read/hear the word BLEUGH you do it. Do NOT hold back. The grosser and more realistic, the better.)

An undercooked wobbly omelette,
spitty bone that a dog won't fetch
a bogy rolled into the carpet
these are the things that make Mum retch

But Mum's never actually sick . . . she just
    makes a noise like this –

BLEUGH! BLEUGH! BLEUGH!

When people bite their nails
or chew on their clothes tags
or reek of old BO
just watch my mother gag
But Mum's never actually sick . . . she just
   makes a noise like this –

BLEUGH! BLEUGH! BLEUGH!

The smell of rancid old butter
the sight of sick on TV
I once saw her BLEUGH in the gutter
from bird poo splodging on me

But Mum wasn't actually sick . . . she just
   made a noise like this –

BLEUGH! BLEUGH! BLEUGH!

Opening a can of cat food
cleaning out the fridge
watching Grandma's frail hands
make a tuna sandwich

But Mum's never actually sick . . . she just
makes a noise like this –

BLEUGH! BLEUGH! BLEUGH!

On a school trip to the farm
she saw the wee stains on the straw
and the horse poo swept to the corner
and the cow snot on the floor

But Mum wasn't actually sick . . . she just
    made a noise like this –

BLEUGH! BLEUGH! BLEUGH!

At a fancy restaurant
she saw a man slice fatty ham
and in the squish of pinky bits
she clamped her mouth with a slam

But Mum wasn't actually sick . . . she just made a
    noise like this –

BLEUGH! BLEUGH! BLEUGH!

A baby's dirty nappy
squishing out on the train
the smell of eggy farts
on the aeroplane

But Mum's never actually sick . . . she just
   makes a noise like this –

BLEUGH! BLEUGH! BLEUGH!

When people lick their knives
or scratch out their eyeball gunk
coffee breath in the morning
smells like the bum of a skunk

But Mum isn't actually sick . . . she just
   makes a noise like this –

BLEUGH! BLEUGH! BLEUGH!

Smushy cereal,
sinking milky in the bowl
Parmesan cheese
stale rotten vegetables

But Mum isn't actually sick . . . she just
   makes a noise like this –

BLEUGH! BLEUGH! BLEUGH!

And a bit more of a noise like this . . .

BLEUGH! BLEUGH! BLEUGH!

and that usually means this . . . quick . . .

Me. Being sick.

My Mum Whispers I Love You Like . . .

I love you like fluffy socks
I love you like new sheets
I love you like a stick of rock
I love you like the sea
I love you like a nectarine
I love you like a hum
I love you like a flying dream
I love you like the sun
I love you like an empty day
I love you like potato
I love you like a takeaway
I love you like tomorrow
I love you like picking scabs
I love you like a sneeze
I love you like late kebab
I love you like blue cheese
I love you like an open fire
I love you like black tea
I love you like peace and quiet

Cuckoo Cuckoo

Cu ck o o
Cu ck o o
Cu ck o
ck o o

I love you like whipped cream
I love you like a new start
I love you like relief
I love you like a nanna loves
a personalised handkerchief
I love you like a belly laugh
I love you like fresh bread
I love you like a rocket blast
I love you like a shed
I love you like I'm cuckoo
I love you like I'm mad
I love you like I never knew
a love I never had
I love you like a hurricane
like tight jeans love bums
I love you like ideas love brains
I love you like a mum.

Cu ck o o
Cu ck o o
Cu ck o
Cu ck o o
Cu ck o o
Cu ck o o
Cu ck o o
Cu ck o o
Cu ck o o
Cu ck o o
Cu ck o o
Cu ck o
Cu ck o o
Cu ck o
Cu ck o —

Cu ck o
Cu ck o o

Cu ck o
Cu ck o o

The Old-Lady-Sitter

I'm starting a business
more of a revolution
something to fix
this backwards evolution

that kids are kids
then this adult intrusion
of weird misfits
and utter confusion.

Yes I know I'm the child
but I'm the mature one round here
because my mum is wild
and I live in constant fear

I don't need a babysitter
to take care of me
I need a MUM-sitter
to give me some relief.

And why are they called *baby*sitters
when a baby they do not sit?
So let's invent *old-lady*-sitters
and see how they like it.

And the kids can go out
and leave Mum with someone else
who can leave food in the fridge
and the keys on the shelf

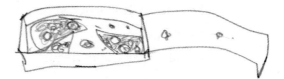

and the kids can wave goodbye
and leave a number *just in case*
whilst Mum sits and cries
and goes red in the face.

There's beer if she needs it
but I'm sure she'll be fine
just keep feeding her tea
or else reach for the wine

and the hours will drag by
for the old-lady-sitter
who will mumble all wired
all tired and bitter

as the Mum will scramble
and want to jump on the bed
and do the sitter a painting
and stick stickers on her head

and the old-lady-sitter will
sit and use the phone
to call up her schoolfriends
or maybe call home

whilst the Mum wants to
maybe just, you know, do a show?
Or a karaoke one-off
or a violin solo
(of which she cannot play).

And good luck at bedtime
because the mum won't close her eyes
she'll just do heavy breathing
and then scream **SURPRISE!**

And it won't be worth the money
and it won't be worth the time.
Babysitting a mummy
is like being punished for a crime.

But wouldn't it be cool
to have at least one night off?
No mum to see to.
No mum to tell off.

So, I'm starting a business.
Problems? Only one.
I just need to ask permission
from my . . . err . . . mum.

My Mum Does Cleaning

Want to know a little bit
of how Mum cleans the house?
She puts an apple in my trainer
and in the fridge a mouse.
There's keys in the oven,
a strainer in the bath,
an iron on the doorstep,
salad down the path.
There's lipstick on the bookshelf,
letters on the floor,
bacon in the sugar pot
and mustard on the door.

There's rats in the TV
acting out a scene,
mould on the windowsill
and she calls *that* clean.
There's baked beans on the taps
and a high heel by the mirror,
skeletons in the bath
and in her scarf a pitta.
There's money in the sofa,
eggs in the bed,
knickers in the toaster,
a bra instead of bread.
There's a toothbrush in the saucepan,
a guitar on the stairs,
a spoon meant for pasta
but it's just covered in hair.
And don't say you've not been warned,
just know when you get there
that by cleaning up Mum means
put stuff everywhere.

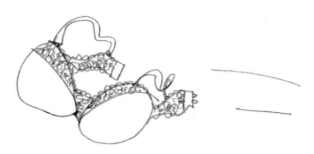

My Mum Does Not Grow Up

W here to go
where to go
to see the grown-ups glump –

Some say
some say
they fill out the train
swelling in a grump.

They eat
they eat
all boring things
with all the treats cut out
I wonder what the grown-ups
have to even moan about?

They run
they run
as in ACTUAL run
and they don't do it for fun.

They drink
they drink
this coffee thing
and then say *ummmm yum.*

They moan
they moan
about their homes
when they're the ones in charge of it.
I wonder where the grown-ups go
to simply get over it?

They talk
they talk
a blah blah blah
a gibbledy gobbledygook.

They dress
they dress
in ugly things
like same-as-everyone suits.

They count
they count
the silly sad things like wrinkles
and money and time
one day they'll look around

and ask how
the clock's wings flew on by

so . . .

Watch Out
Watch Out
all grown-ups now
watch out, I'll tell you now!

The trap
the trap
could happen to you
and so you must break out.

The trick
the trick
is the opposite
and quite easy to work out . . .
Don't grow up at all, says Mum,
just keep on growing down.
Just don't grow up at all, says Mum,
just keep on growing d
                      o

                         w

                            n.

My Mum's Allergic

Some people are allergic to bumble bees
some allergic to nuts
you might be allergic to dairy or wheat
to perfume or to dust

Some are allergic to bubble bath
some the scruff of cat fur
some are intolerant to detergent
and can flare from washing powder

But my mum has an allergy
and it is a very serious worry
no matter what she says or does
she just cannot say sorry

The symptoms are severe
side-effects cause for concern
if a sorry even comes near her
Mum's skin will itch and burn

You don't want to see what happens, Son
it will give you quite the fright
so I don't say sorry to anyone
which means I'm always mostly right

But very occasionally
on the rare chance she might
she sometimes gives me a small sorry
(but only to be polite)

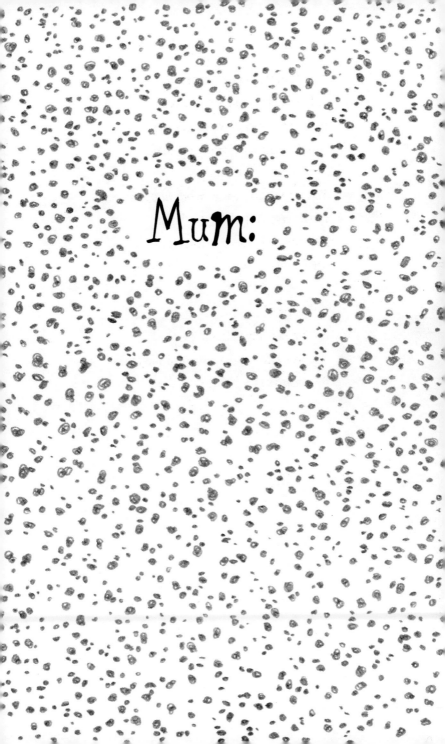

Mum:

My Mum Says Don't Be a Spoiled Brat

DON'T be a **BRAT THAT** is
spoiled
and **CRASS**
exploding like
boiling
hot oil
on **MASS**
you can't be THAT
or I'll send you **BACK**
as quick as a **FLASH**
to the shop of spoiled brats.

My Mum Does Road Rage

Watch it you **NUTBAG**
you wheel of rolling cheese
you old **hag**
you **nail snag**
you bumped into **ME!**
You beeped me
you **BEEP BEEP**
I'll smash up
your **BIG** jeep
don't call me a **BEEP BEEP**
or I'll BEEPING freak!
How dare you?
You **monster**
you think
you're a **rock star?**
You skull face
you scarecrow
you goggle-eyed weirdo
the green light means
GO

GO
but
YOU
go
so
S-L-O-W
SLOW
AGH
NO NO
don't beep **ME**
YOU **BEEP BEEPING**
BEEP
BEEP
I'll call the police, see?

Then you'll be sorry.
You thumped up
my bumper
I'll jump start
your **dump** car
the old lump
is one hump
from meeting
the dumpster.

I WANT A PARTY!

I **want** to have a party
hip hip hooray
I want a clown to come along
someone to paint my face

I'm gonna **SO** have a party
a bouncy castle too
pin the tail on the donkey
and eat multi-coloured food

I'm **going** to throw a party
pass the parcel with my mates
and rip all the paper off
when it's not my turn to play

Let's dance at my party, **yeah?**
to a game of musical chairs
but not sit down when I'm meant to
and then shout **'IT'S NOT FAIR!'**

I'm going to perform at my party
to songs *I* only like
and do a bit of wrestling
and freestyling on my bike

I'm going to be *wild* at my party
and make it all about **ME**
and be the centre of attention and
throw a tantrum like I'm three

I'll be bossy at **MY** party
and tell everyone what's what
and stack my gifts into a tower
and get everything I want

I'm like the **PARTY** of my own **PARTY**
I'm like a volcano about to erupt
lucky ***me*** for inviting *myself*
so nice of *me* to show up

I *might* cry at my party
and get 'over-excited' again
and people will say I'm just 'tired'
and say sorry to my friends

120

I'll get angry at my party
and selfish and mean and rude
and tell everyone what I think of them
and chuck up cake in the loo

My Mum Orders a Takeaway

Where's **the** pen?
where's the thing
the thingy the thing
the menu to the thingy thing
punch the number in the –
this pen doesn't work, again –
~~stupid~~
~~thing~~
pass me that lipstick
then
I'll have to write in that.
Ooo yeah hi
hi so much
I'd like to place an order –
I want the crispy things
with the things stuffed in
it's a dry thing – ah – yes –
with the chilli? That's the one.
And I want those things, the
long things

with the crispy bits
and the –
ah you got it. That's it.
I want the **round** things
like spacehopper *blobs*
floating in the orange sauce
and
the green mermaid hair
fried and *tonged*
and the triangles of
sesame mountains
mixed with breakfast toast.
Let's have those white polar bear ears
that melt and frazzle on your tongue
I want the wormy ribbons
with the silver snail onions
and the black lagoon of beans
and the giants feet
and the mini trees
in the **salty** sea
and the teeth
of a baby pug
with the egg that looks like
chewing gum

123

and the sleeping spring bugs
in their deep-fried rugs
and the melted gold moon that
glug, glug, glugs . . .
and add to that
the pancakes that quack

now

do you think you can read that back?

My Mum Gives Advice

*Y*ou just do your best my love
that's all you have to do
you get on with being you
and I'll get on with loving you

if it seems too big to climb
just find another way through
you just get on with being you
and I'll get on with loving you

you just do your best my love
don't care what people think
just gargle others' opinions
with mouthwash down the sink

you just keep being a lovely one
give everyone a chance
don't take things too seriously
and make every moment last

treat others as you'd treat yourself
with kindness and lots of love
and remember almost anything
can be fixed up with a hug

sticks and stones and all that love
take with a pinch of salt
sometimes bad things just happen
and it isn't anybody's fault

BUT if a meanie's mean to you
I'll tell you what I'll do
I'll **ROAST** that weenie meanie
with green beans for a stew

I'll mince their brains
    with vinegar
and **MUNCH** their
    eyes on bread

and **GUZZLE UP** their
    HORRID hearts
with soldiers and
    dippy egg

and if that meanie's *still* mean to you
I'll tell you what I'll do
I'll give myself a bellyache
and make them eat the puke

so you just do your best my love
that's all you have to do
and let me be the only one
that can be mean for you.

My Mum Makes Everything Sound Easy When It's Actually Not

On your bike
hop to the shops
nip to the station
drop by the post box
skip to the bakers
pop upstairs
do me a quick favour
ta love, cheers
chuck on some dinner
go on . . .
tip me out a tea
jot out a letter
float oversees
buzz me a message
scoot off to Spain
pick me a present . . .

just . . . *read* my mind again

pass that exam
WIN that prize
knock up a flan
FLY twice as high
Just **PLAY** the guitar
Just **LEARN** life is breezy
because nothing is hard
if you act like it's easy.

My Mum Explains Stuff

I think we need to have a talk.
The talk, the talk, the talk.

The one about how babies
are delivered by a stork.

I think it's time we had THE talk.
The talk, the talk, the talk . . .

It's like baking a cake, you see,
that needs ingredients and love

a little pinch of sugar
and a fireproof oven glove

a smothering of jam
and a dustpan for the crumbs

and the proof is in the pudding
when the making is all done.

Hmmm . . . let me try again . . .

You see giants live in mountains
high up in the clouds

and pour errr . . . *baby water . . .* like a fountain
onto mums' heads raining down

and the water is magic
and when it hits the ground

a baby lies and waits
until it maybe gets found?

*No. Not convinced . . . OK . . . this is harder than I
thought . . .*

Alright . . . I'll try again . . .

A unicorn and a princess
set into the forest wild

they travel for months
until they find a child

hiding in the bushes
in a blanket, in a pile

is a perfect chubby baby
with a perfect happy smile.

Oh, that's terrible . . . no that's not it at all . . .
OK . . .

It's actually in a cup of tea
a secret remedy

that once in a mummy's tummy
can make a baby

it's a special brew
that tastes like poo but the strength is crazy

and that's how you do it, Son,
you just need the recipe.

You don't believe me?

OK . . .

When two people love each other
they tend to argue

they really love each other
but they still probably argue
and one will make a point
but it probably won't get through

it's nothing to do with baby making
it's just a fact that's true.

So you know about that talk.
The talk, the talk, the talk.

You were right all along,
babies are delivered by storks.

I'm so glad we did the talking,
the talk between you and me.
But that was exhausting . . .
I need a cup of tea.

My Mum Has No Space Left in Her Heart

R ight.
That's it. It's full.
She said
I officially have no space left.
All my heart is taken up
with love for you in my chest.
I try to love a something new
but it just doesn't stand a chance
as the love for you I cannot undo
or try to make room in my heart.
I try to maybe like you less
pull out your baby flaws
but my ribcage only bursts a bit
as my heart fills up some more.
So my soul
is swelling so
with a smattering burst of stars
I couldn't even love
another you
as there just isn't the space in my heart.

My Mum: *Little Life*
(PLEASE USE A MAGNIFYING GLASS)

*L*ittle life

little life

is the only life you need

a little life

with the ease

of doing as you please

don't worry

if it seems you could

get murdered by a sneeze

you act out your little life

with little you as the lead

then little you

can smile and breathe

and be happy and be free

as the littler the life

you live

... the bigger the peace of mind for me.

My Mum: BIG LIFE

*S*crap that.

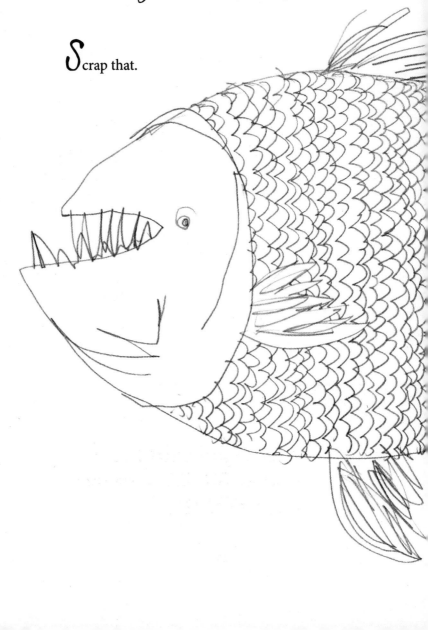

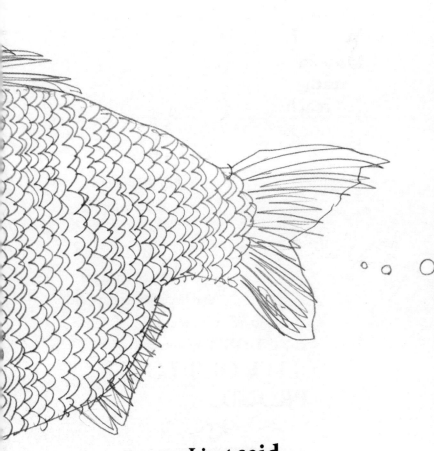

everything **I just said . . .**
take it into a **BIG BALL**, **smush** it
up and **STOMP** on it.

141

You have to live a **BIG LIFE**
you have to S-T-R-E-T-C-H your hands and fingers
W   **I**   **D**   **E**

and reach

reach

reach

for

surprise

like the ocean

reaches for the

beach

and snatch wishes

with an open net

and bring home big fishes

to feed your mind on

and **DON'T** apologise

LIVE OUT LOUD
PROUD

and upside-down

and do things your way

even if it's the opposite way

from the crowd

ALWAYS BE

OUT LOUD
OUT LOUD

it must be a big life

'one big life to go!'

that's fast and tropical and

adventurous and exotic

one that's never going to slow

a life that's **ambitious**

and *delicious*

and gives you a certain glow

wear red cheeks

everywhere you go

and a grin that speaks

of the big life that only you know

nothing is ever **too big an ask**

nothing is too tall

for you, my child, are only young

but never let your life be small.

My Mum's Son

When you were in my tummy
says Mum
the world rumbled something **HUGE**
that day
I knew things would never be the same again.
A hero
was growing in my belly
carving his name into the stars
and you would be a carnival
a tornado
a tremendous rocket that could never come too
soon
wearing a fantastic rucksack
with excellent news on your back
and a smile that could keep me awake for years.

And all of the love I knew before
seemed to shatter
and feel a bit embarrassed
because soon I would know you.
I would want to eat your hands
in between two slices of bread
in a sandwich that would never end.

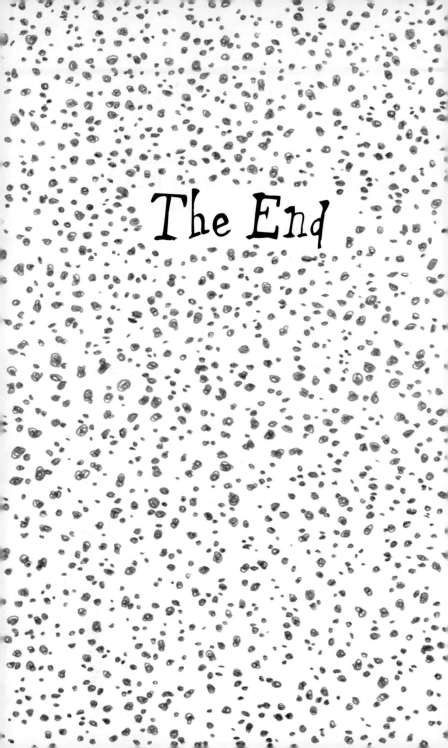

The End

From Laura's Mum:

One day you look in a mirror and are happy with the person smiling back but when it **REALLY** matters an annoying bird has built a nest in your hair and drawn big spots on your face.

One day pink, sparkles, tigers, mud, felt-tips, loop da loops and jumping on the sofa make you happy, but sometimes that was yesterday.

Basically when you're not quite grown-up being alive is a giant, scary, fun, adventure . . .

I thank Laura for never ever asking or expecting me to become a grown-up mum.